Freight Train

Donald Crews

A Mulberry Paperback Book
New York

First Mulberry Edition, 1992.
10 9 8 7 6 5

Library of Congress Cataloging in Publication Data. Crews, Donald. Freight train. Summary: Brief text and illustrations trace the journey of a colorful train as it goes through tunnels, by cities, and over trestles. [1. Railroads–Trains–Pictorial works. 2. Colors. 3. Picture books] I. Title. PZ7.C8682Fr [E] 78-2303 ISBN 0-688-11701-5

With due respect to Casey Jones, John Henry, The Rock Island Line, and the countless freight trains passed and passing the big house in Cottondale

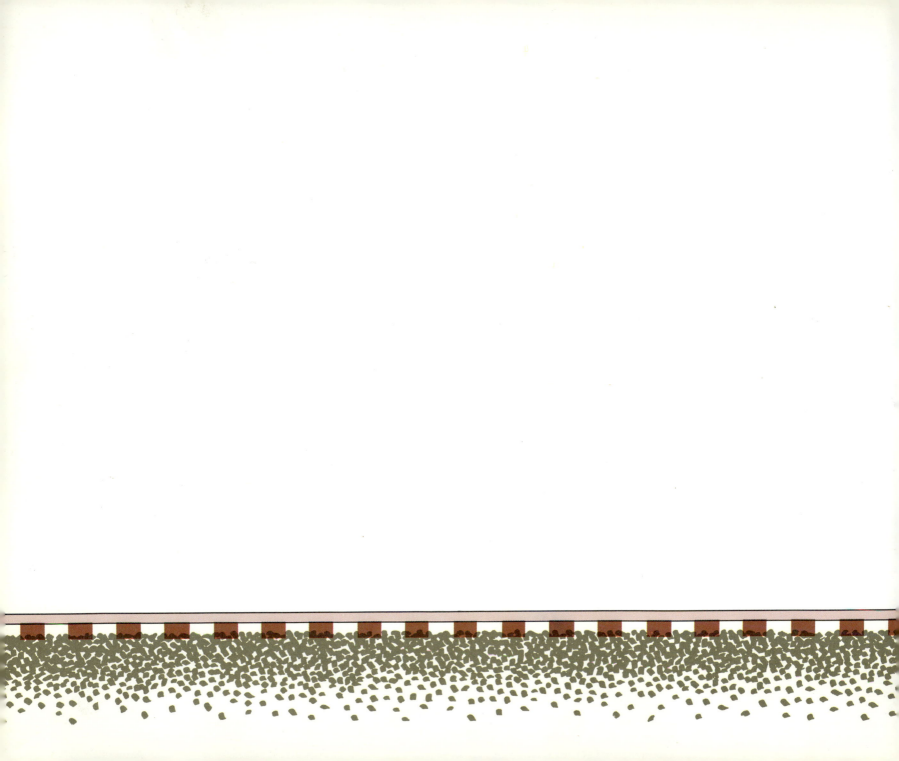

A train runs across this track.

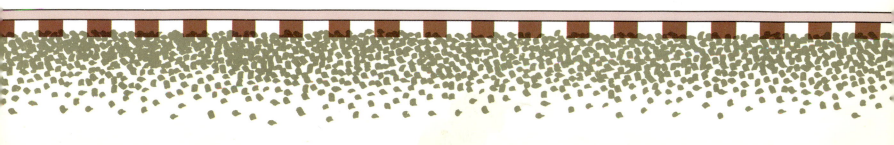

**Red caboose
at the back**

**Orange
tank
car
next**

**Yellow
hopper car**

Green cattle car

Blue gondola car

**Purple
box car**

a Black
tender and

a Black
steam engine.

N&A

Freight train.

Moving.

Going through tunnels

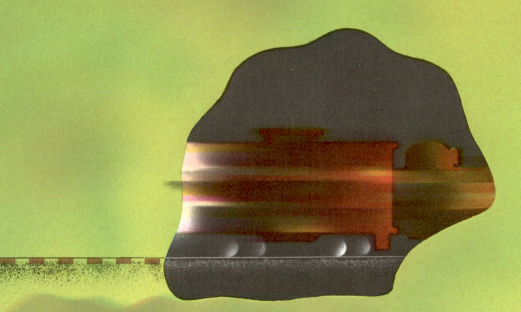

Going by cities

Crossing trestles.

Moving in darkness.

Moving in daylight.
Going, going...

gone.